WHITE WONDERFUL WINTER!

by Elaine W. Good
Illustrated by Susie Shenk Wenger

Good Books®
Intercourse, PA 17534

White Wonderful Winter!
Copyright © 1991 by Good Books, Intercourse, PA 17534
International Standard Book Number:
1-56148-018-5
Library of Congress Catalog Card Number:
91-74052

Library of Congress Cataloging-in-Publication Data

Good, Elaine W., 1944-
  White wonderful winter! / by Elaine W. Good : illustrated by Susie Shenk Wenger.
    p.   cm.
  Summary: A boy who lives on a farm delights in the pleasures of white, wonderful winter, but when spring comes he is glad to greet the new season.
  ISBN 1-56148-018-5 : $12.95
  [1. Winter—Fiction. 2. Seasons—Fiction. 3. Farm life—Fiction.] I. Wenger, Susie Shenk, 1956- 1ll. II. Title.
PZ7.G5996Wh   1991   91-74052
[E]—dc20   CIP
                                                      AC

"There's winter in the air," Daddy says one evening as we sit down to eat supper. "It's nippy out there." Brandy seems to agree because he begs to come in to our cozy kitchen.

White, wonderful winter!

It might be cloudy and cold outside but our kitchen is bright and warm. Today I am helping Mommy bake bread. While she kneads the dough I drive my toy tractors through a pile of flour.

White, wonderful winter!

I need help to get dressed this morning. It's so cold I have to wear longjohns like Daddy's under my jeans.

White, wonderful winter!

The water in the chickens' fountain is frozen. They are so thirsty they come running when we dump out the ice and pour in fresh water.
White, wonderful winter!

Christmas is coming! Mommy and Daddy needed help with their Christmas letters so I drew pictures for Grandma and Grandpa. Mommy lets me put the letters in the mailbox.

White, wonderful winter!

Rain and wind and cold and ice all come with winter. But the best is when it snows! David plowed the lane so the milk truck could come in, then we built a snowman and went sledding in the meadow.

White, wonderful winter!

Daddy and I hike down by the creek. We can tell many stories from the animal tracks in the snow. We find tracks of rabbits, a raccoon, a fox, a skunk, an opossum and a pheasant!

White, wonderful winter!

Bright sunshine makes Mommy feel like she can hang the wash outside
today. The cold air freezes it as fast as she hangs it up.
White, wonderful winter!

Mommy put the Christmas wrapping paper on the dining room table. Now every evening I have to stay out of there while someone is wrapping presents. Mommy understands how I feel so she mixes up some cookies and we bake them.

White, wonderful winter!

On Christmas Eve Daddy takes me along to the barn to help give hay to the cows. The hay swishes, the cows munch, frost crackles on the windows and Daddy hugs me as we listen.

White, wonderful winter!

"Merry Christmas!" Caroline hollered up the stairs when she and Daddy came in from milking the cows. We all hurried to the living room to open our presents before going to Grandpa's for Christmas dinner. The big cousins take us younger ones along ice skating in the afternoon.

White, wonderful winter!

One clear night Daddy shows me the stars called Orion. The easiest ones to see are the three that make Orion's belt. I can always find them over our barn roof.

White, wonderful winter!

Mommy and I went shopping for wool so she can make me new mittens.
When we are done Joanna takes us out to her barn so I can hold a baby
lamb. Wool on sheep and wool on me!

White, wonderful winter!

Sometimes winter isn't just snowy or icy. It's also muddy! Boots and tricycle wheels make great tracks in the mud. "Boys and mud go together, like summertime and sunny weather," sings Mommy as she helps me into clean clothes.

White, (brown!) wonderful winter!

I don't know what Mommy means! She says winter is never long enough! She wants to finish my quilt before she has to plant the peas. I am tired of wearing longjohns and jackets!

Winter is wonderful, but

I can't wait for SPRING!